Louella
and the
Librarian

Written by Christine Ricci-McNamee

Illustrated by Patrick Regan

Leaning Rock Press,
Gales Ferry, CT

Leaning Rock Press, LLC
Gales Ferry, CT 06335
leaningrockpress@gmail.com
www.leaningrockpress.com

978-1-950323-33-3, Hardcover
978-1-950323-36-4, Softcover

Library of Congress Control Number: 2022917943

Publisher's Cataloging-in-Publication Data
(Prepared by Cassidy Cataloguing's PCIP Service)

Names: Ricci-McNamee, Christine M., author. | Regan, Patrick, 1994- illustrator.

Title: Louella and the librarian / by: Christine Ricci-McNamee ; illustrated by Patrick Regan.

Description: Gales Ferry, CT : Leaning Rock Press, [2022] | Interest age level: 003-010. | Summary: Louella, a curious eight-year-old girl, had never been to the library. She had heard about this "magical place" from her mother who had told her stories about Margie the Librarian. Join Louella on her adventure as she gets her first library card, meets new friends and discovers the world through books.--Publisher.

Identifiers: ISBN: 978-1-950323-33-3 (hardcover) | 978-1-950323-36-4 (softcover) | LCCN: 2022917943

Subjects: LCSH: Libraries--Juvenile fiction. | Librarians--Juvenile fiction. | Books and reading--Juvenile fiction. | Learning by discovery--Juvenile fiction. | Library cards--Juvenile fiction. | Friendship --Juvenile fiction. | Children with disabilities--Juvenile fiction. | Storytelling--Juvenile fiction. | Children's libraries--Activity programs--Juvenile fiction. | CYAC: Libraries--Fiction. | Librarians--Fiction. | Books and reading--Fiction. | Friendship--Fiction. | Children with disabilities--Fiction. | Storytelling--Fiction. | Children's libraries--Fiction. | BISAC: JUVENILE FICTION / Books & Libraries. | JUVENILE FICTION / Social Themes / Friendship.

Classification: LCC: PZ7.1.R522 Lou 2022 | DDC: [E]--dc23

Printed in the United States of America

I worked as a Library Aide throughout my high school years and some of college. It was there I met a very special woman, Mary LaFollette.

Mary was an assistant Librarian of the Boston Public Library for over 50 years and a loyal employee. Although she never attended library school, she knew who wrote every title and where they could be found. Mary would sit at her wooden desk for hours, lovingly repairing torn book jackets, spines and tattered pages. She would always have a fresh batch of handmade bookmarks ready for patrons.

Everyone knew Mary. She had a jolly laugh and was always smiling. She would decorate the library's windows, doors, and bulletin boards for every holiday. At Christmas time, she would hold an open house so that the patrons could gather together.

Mary has since passed away, but I will always remember her fondly.

This book is dedicated in her memory.

Louella, an only child, was sitting on her bedroom floor playing with her dog Twiggy, a mixed breed, brown and black lab. She then heard her mother calling.

"Come on Louella, it's time to go. Don't forget your sweater. It's chilly out."

"Okay, Mom. I'll be right there," She answered.

"You stay here, Twiggy," Louella said. "Mom and I will be right back. We're going to the library. No dogs allowed." Twiggy, as if he understood, jumped on the bed and rested his head on the pillow.

Louella was excited. In all of her eight years, she had never once been to the library.

Her mother loved to read and was always bringing home books for Louella that Margie, the Librarian, had picked out for her. Louella couldn't wait to meet Margie. Her mother was always talking about how Margie was always laughing and how she would help children select out books for their school projects. Margie, her mother said, would even save the latest releases of new books for her loyal patrons in a secret place behind the front counter.

Louella also loved to read. When there was no one to play with, books helped to pass the time.

Today Louella was going to get her very own library card.

Holding her mother's hand, Louella walked through the fallen leaves to the local branch library that was only a few doors down from where she lived.

Her next-door neighbor was outside raking in the front yard.

"Hi, Mr. Enos." Louella smiled and waved to the tall, thin, silver-haired, elderly man.

"Why hello there, Louella. Where are you ladies off to today."

"My mother is taking me on my first visit to the library," Louella answered excitedly.

"That's very nice," Mr. Enos replied. "Have Fun!"

"Thanks. I will. Bye!" Louella shouted and waved.

The library was a square brick building on the corner of the street. It had huge windows with fall leaves taped to them for decoration. A white sign hung from one of its corners and the words PUBLIC LIBRARY were etched into the concrete above two massive, wooden entry doors.

6

As soon as her mother opened the door and they walked up the stairs, Louella knew she had entered a magical place. At the top of the stairs was a huge wooden desk. It was the biggest desk Louella had ever seen. It was surrounded by rows and rows of books that stretched all the way to the ceiling. She had never seen so many books.

To the right of the big desk was a smaller wooden desk covered with stacks of books, jars of glue, stickers, and colored construction paper.

From behind the stack of books, Louella could see a woman brushing glue onto a book spine. The woman had short brown curly hair and a round jolly face. She reminded Louella of Mrs. Claus. She had on navy blue slacks, an orange top with a hot pink beaded necklace, and matching hot pink earrings. Her glasses hung on a beaded chain around her neck.

"Hello, Jean," the woman said to my mother with a smile. "Who is this little gem?"

"Hi Margie," my mother replied. "This is my daughter Louella. It's her first visit to the library."

"Well, hello there. I'm Margie, the Librarian," the jolly woman said, shaking Louella's hand. "It's nice to meet you. Let me show you around, and then we'll get you a library card. Would you like some punch and cookies?" On the table next to the desk was a round glass punch bowl and a tray of sugar cookies.

"No, thank you," Louella answered shyly.

"Come with me, little lady," Margie said. "I'll take you to the Children's Room." Louella couldn't believe that there was a room just for her.

The Children's Room was on the left side of the giant desk. Louella could hear the whispers and giggles of excited children. There were round wooden tables, small wooden chairs, and rows of low bookcases that even Louella could reach. Louella knew she was going to like this place.

"You are just in time for story hour," Margie said to Louella. "Now you sit right here with the other children and we will begin shortly."

Louella sat down at one of the small round wooden tables. Next to her was a boy with braces on both of his legs. Louella noticed that no one was talking to him.

"Hi, my name is Louella. What's your name?" she said to the little red-haired, freckled-faced boy.

"My name is Andy," he replied. "I live around the corner with my foster family. Where do you live?" he asked curiously.

"I live down the street with my parents and dog, Twiggy," Louella answered. "Do you like the library? It sure seems like a fun place," she asked as she looked around at all of the other boys and girls reading, working on computers, and doing fun craft projects. Today they were making leaves traced from construction paper with glitter.

"It's okay," he replied in a shy quiet voice, shrugging with his head down. "No one really talks to me."

"I'll be your friend," Louella said. "And Twiggy will too!"

"I'd like that," Andy responded with a smile.

Suddenly they heard a booming voice.

"Okay, children it's time for story hour!" It was Margie.

"Everyone put their chairs in a circle. Today's story is about a mysterious house."

The children all gathered around her as Margie began to read.

When story hour was over, Margie took Louella's hand and said, "Now it's time to pick out the first book you can check out on your own."

She took Louella over to a stack of books in the Children's Room.

"I think you might like some of these. Take a look through them and see which one you'd like."

Louella's eyes got big as she looked at the books. All of them seemed to be about little girls her age with animals. In the stack nearby, she could see a boy looking through books about trucks and baseball. Louella liked baseball and trucks but would much rather read about animals.

After she'd picked out a book, she went up to Margie at the big desk and showed her what she had selected.

"Great choice, Louella. I think you will enjoy it," Margie said with a smile.

She then typed Louella's name and address into the computer and handed her a card to sign. It was her official library card.

Louella was so happy. Finally, she could take out books by herself, just like her mother.

Margie explained that a book could be borrowed for two weeks and then would have to be returned by the due date on the back pocket. Louella could then take out another book or even two, three, or four more. This was so exciting!

Margie also gave Louella a handmade bookmark she made for all the patrons. It was cut out of construction paper with a pumpkin sticker stapled to the top.

"This place is great," Louella thought to herself. "I even get presents!"

Louella said goodbye to Andy, and they promised to keep in touch. Then she was reunited with her mother, who had been reading and relaxing over coffee and tea with the other mothers and fathers in the adult room.

"Goodbye, Margie," her mother said as they left the library. "Thank you for all your help."

"It was my pleasure," Margie replied. "You have a lovely daughter. I hope to see you both again soon."

"Don't worry, Margie. You will." Louella said as she happily skipped down the stairs. "The library is fun!"

Author

Christine Ricci-McNamee is an honors graduate of Salem State University in Salem, MA where she earned her B.A. in English/ Written Communications. She is a certified Paralegal and resides in East Boston, in her childhood home. When she is not busy running the family businesses, she enjoys walks with her dog Winston, traveling, spending time with family and friends, reading, photography, gardening and of course writing.

Christine was the winner of the Presidential Arts Scholarship in Creative Writing at Salem State. She also was an American Poetry Association Poet of Merit, as well as the winner of the Boston Public Library Scholar's Award.

Her poetry has appeared in several anthologies such as the American Collegiate Poets, the American Poetry Association Anthology, the American Anthology of Contemporary Poetry and in "*A Time To Be Free*"; a poetry anthology published by Quill Books.

Christine has also written two other books:

Flames of Feeling, a delightful collection of poems for children and young adults on various themes.

Logan and the Lost Luggage, with themes of kindness, friendship, landmarks/ geography, and diversity that will spark wonderful conversations between parents and children or teachers and students.

**Christine can be reached through her Instagram at:
eastie_author**

Illustrator

Patrick Regan is an illustrator, graphic designer, and motion graphic designer from New London, Connecticut. He had an ambitious and creative drive from an early age. Growing up, he spent countless hours at the kitchen table bringing his imagination to life through drawing, and in doing so, he created and destroyed hundreds of fictional characters and universes.

Ultimately, this led to his enrollment at the Hartford Art School where he began to refine his skills. He received a BFA in illustration in 2016. Since graduating, Patrick has worked as a motion graphic designer in the video marketing industry, creating animated commercials for TV, video streaming services, and web. He also has experience illustrating beer cans, children's books, book covers, and album art, as well as designing logos, menus, tattoos, book layouts, T-shirts, and other merchandise.

When not working on commissioned projects, Patrick is busy designing, illustrating, animating, and bringing to life his own fantasy world projects. He enjoys collecting comics and vinyl, reading, and spending time at the beach.

**Patrick can be reached at:
patrick_regan@sbcglobal.net**

**His portfolio can be viewed at:
faireharbourart.com**

The Library

by Christine Ricci-McNamee

A place of wonder and fascination
with books that contain lots of valuable information,
books on music, art, magic, travel and cooking.
You can spend a lot of time there just looking.

There are books about famous people,
on leaders like Martin Luther King
and writers like Washington Irving.

Books are returned and more are checked out.
That is what the library is all about.

(Excerpt from the author's first book
of children's poetry called. "Flames of Feeling.")